The Strange Case of Rachel K

Also by Rachel Kushner

Telex from Cuba
The Flamethrowers

THE STRANGE CASE
OF RACHEL K

Rachel Kushner

A NEW DIRECTIONS BOOK

Grateful acknowledgment is made to *Bomb*, *Soft Targets*, and *Descant*, where these stories first appeared.

Manufactured in the United States of America
New Directions Books are printed on acid-free paper.
First published as a New Directions book in 2015
Design by Erik Rieselbach

Library of Congress Cataloging-in-Publication Data
Kushner, Rachel.
[Short stories. Selections]
The strange case of Rachel K / Rachel Kushner. — First edition.
pages ; cm
ISBN 978-0-8112-2421-5 (hardcover : acid-free paper)
I. Title.
PS3611.U7386A6 2015
813'.6—dc23   2014032864

10 9 8 7 6 5 4 3 2 1

New Directions Books are published for James Laughlin
by New Directions Publishing Corporation
80 Eighth Avenue, New York 10011

Contents

Preface

One day ten years ago I sat down and for approximately twenty hours read an enormous book on the history of so-called civilization, a work of seductive details (the Peruvians believed the world was a box with a ridged top, the Egyptians that it was an egg) and an Occidental outlook, critical of every religion and ideology except the dogma of progress itself. Its successive assertions— "People who could agree on few other facts about the remote regions of the earth somehow agreed on the geography of the afterworld" and "More appealing than knowledge itself was the feeling of knowing"—were like the galloping of horses to me. My heart beat with their hooves. I wanted to run alongside, but with my own version of discovery and progress. I did so, by writing "The Great Exception."

* * *

"The Strange Case of Rachel K" was something else, the name of a Cuban film made in the early 1970s, during Cuba's great revolutionary film renaissance (not documented in big books about world progress). I have never seen it. It is one filmmaker's interpretation of a vague historical record concerning a real person named Rachel K, a 1930s courtesan found murdered in a hotel room. I followed an instinct to build my own interpretation of her, making the record less vague, more specific, and procuring for her, as foil, another real historical figure, Christian de la Mazière, whose dubious and fascinating personal history is recounted in Marcel Ophüls's documentary `. I started from the presumption that Rachel K definitely would not die, at least not in the way prescribed by the lessons of history. You might notice that she shares my name; I did too. Writers who have rejected logic and science , those galloping horses, take a different path, through coincidence, the cunning of reason, and mystical signs pointing in the direction that is to be taken.

* * *

"Debouchment" was written under some kind of spell, when the soldiers of the mind came out from their hidden posts, armed and unafraid, self-organized. If I could have written an entire book with the same density and pauses as that one short piece, I would have. Since I did not, this is what I have of its kind.

LOS ANGELES, 2014

THE GREAT EXCEPTION

1

I don't care that the earth's shadow eclipses the moon, said the Admiral. I have seen terrific irregularity with mine own eyes, and have been forced to the sensible conclusion that this earth is not round as some wrongly insist, but the shape of a pear, or violin.

A thousand years before the Admiral made his daring proclamation and charted his course on this violin-shaped earth, people thought it was flat like a discus. Until the Greek Cartographer spoke out, claiming it was round like an orange. He'd drawn standard aesthetic divisions on his planisphere, a flattened version of his round earth. The first set of lines he called "latitude." And the second set, trickier than the first, "longitude." But his finest moment, his greatest act of self-control, had been to leave parts of his map blank. The Cartographer was later forgotten, his maps lost like dreams that are lost upon waking, lingering only as faint unglimpsable residues. Seafarers, with no reliable guide by which to brave the open Ocean, paddled and were wind-scooted along in landlocked, salted waters. For navigation, they dead reckoned and used wind roses—radiating lines of sixteen focal points, ornate foliations that indicated air currents but varied according to the size and dimensions of the map, so that no two maps, even of one place, were ever alike. The Cartographer was eventually remembered, but by then the forgetting had been sustained so long that no one could read Greek. The epic after the Cartographer's planisphere reigned and before it reigned again—forgotten and then discovered but unreadable—was known as the Great Interruption. It lasted one thousand years.

Exploring is an undertaking of the brain. The pioneering Portuguese Navigator was one lonely man, thinking. His name was Henry. He wore a hair shirt. He died a virgin. The Portuguese, not waylaid like the rest of Europe by bloody wars, by the Hundred Years one and the other called Roses, were free to daydream. Their country faced the ocean, not the Sea-in-the-Midst-of-the-Land. This orientation gave them a taste for the formless and unfathomable, and Portuguese sailors went south toward Africa, the massive continent with friendly and also unfriendly inhabitants. But their polestar sank as they went, and so they rigged up a kind of crude latitude. They wagered on uncharted courses, and flung themselves into the Watery Unknown.

With Henry's sacrifices and his intuition there were advances. With each advance, the locating and charting of Places, the Pure Unknown was molested, and the mental bravery in revering Nothingness leaked away. Charting courses in the mind came before charting courses in the sea. The Great Exception (shortly after the Great Interruption) was the finding of the Americas, which happened on the earth before it happened in men's minds.

When the Admiral went to Her Highness to explain his astounding insight that the earth was shaped like a pear or violin, and to request the gold for his expedition, he was accidentally drunk from too much wine, and drunk as well on the heady vapors of hubris and conviction. Flushed and inspired, he got on his knee and spirited the story with more zing. He impromptu scrapped the violin thing and told Her Highness that the earth was the shape of a woman's breast. He said the Breast had a protrusion at the Orient, where he wanted to sail, where the water grew warm and tumultuous. The nipple, he said, locking his onyx eyes to her green ones, tracing a breast in the air with his slim-fingered, Portuguese hands. Slim fingers he couldn't resist adorning with the ring the Cardinal had given him for luck, with a cross so large and yellow diamonds so sharply cut, that he'd scratched himself with it more than once.

"Pious excess" would be one way to classify the jewels the Cardinal preferred, to wear and to give to explorers before they set sail. It might have been that the Cardinal had hoped the Admiral would think of him, as he wore the enormous and pointy ring. But the Admiral had thought only of the Queen, or more specifically, the

16

Queen's breast, which he'd all but touched, tracing its curve and pretending to trace the earth's curve. But that had only been a moment. An instrumental moment. The Admiral did not think in the manner that either the Queen or the Cardinal or most people did, of bodies and of desire. He was driven by entirely different impulses, which is why he was an explorer.

With Royal approval, the Admiral set sail toward the Breast's dark and uncharted areola, where the waters grew warm and tumultuous. Never mind the astrolabe, the sextant, the compass or the precious lodestone the Admiral guarded to remagnetize the compass, should it weaken. He navigated most faithfully by a special form of reasoning, by which the world—possibly unmappable—conformed to the Admiral's mental map of a well-shaped Breast. The places he encountered turned out to have been just the places he meant to have encountered. Such as the absurdly large slab of land that appeared at the Breast's protrusion, before he reached the Orient. A crenulated green continent with volcanic lakes and snow-capped mountains. En route to the green crenulated slab, he floated toward a smallish and exquisite island the shape of a sardine or eyebrow, with riotous colors and flowering trees, humid and fresh. He anchored in one of its eastern harbors, whose shore was paved with pulverized white diamonds. Beyond the white diamond shore was a thick curtain of monochrome green vines. The Admiral parted the vines and called out, "Hello?"

He named the place Kuba, which is what the natives—who appeared to greet him from beyond the green jungle drapery—said it was called. And what the Germans, fond of the letter K, still call it. The Admiral napped in a hammock strung between a palm and a paw-paw, tired after such a long journey, lulled by the syncopated crash of waves and the sultry and healthful air, happy in his own genius and exactly where he wanted to be. True beauty and the unknown are alike, in having no precedents. You recognize them when you see them, if you have such a gift of seeing. Numeric calculations are no match for life's unrest. Far superior is knowing the world is a pear, a violin, a breast. By such poetic and razor precision, the Admiral mapped an unmappable world.

2

They cooked his toes separate from the rest of the stew. With the toes severed from the feet, the Admiral could not tromp inland and subjugate the island. He couldn't tromp inland anyhow, because they'd punctured his body with arrows dipped in deadly machineel sap. When the natives attacked, the Admiral had instinctively pulled out his shaving mirror and reflected sunlight at them. But the natives were not as crude as the Admiral had suspected. They'd known how to make mirrors since the Neolithic age, with self-polishing obsidian. The Admiral was wading through a sulfuric bog, trying to run away, when they ambushed him. Soon after, his body simmered over a fire of mangrove charcoal, in a soup that bubbled and steamed. They weren't driven to eat him out of hunger—this was the Tropics, bountiful with sea animals and wild fruits, and the living was easy. When the meat was tender, the Tribe Taster had a bite. He said, in a language now lost, that the Admiral tasted like rubber bands. Two men and a boy dumped the enormous pot on its side and bones and meat and broth sluiced onto the red clay earth. They carefully extinguished the fire and vacated their cooksite. What was dumped from the pot, leftovers spoiling and reheating in the sunlight, was eaten by wild pigs. The French Poet, who came later in this history, believed that noxious animals were the embodiment of man's evil thoughts. This man's evil thoughts lapped him up, flesh, femur, and marinade.

The queen was anxious for the Admiral's return. Not only for the feedback, which meant bounty from the exploration, in a time when this imperialist meaning was the only meaning the term "feedback" had, but to satisfy her desire. The pomp and expense of the Admiral's voyage to the Orient had seemed a kind of elaborate foreplay between the two of them. In circling the earth the Admiral was circling her breast with his slim, Portuguese fingers. And the circling of the breast was only a prologue to other, more irreversible acts. Meanwhile, the Cardinal had forgotten all about the Admiral, preoccupied with other jewelry, sharper and more elaborate, for other dandies, braver and more attentive than the Admiral had been, who never even thanked the Cardinal for his yellow diamond ring.

The Queen was washed-over with desire, remembering the Admiral's shining black eyes, his broom-heavy lashes sweeping down and then up again as he'd requested the gold. The Admiral had put his head in her lap after he told her, passionately, of the earth's true shape. She'd resisted the urge to push his face into the bunting and toile of her skirt. She thought of him and squeezed her legs together. The King asked her what she was doing and she said nothing. For days on end she crossed her legs and squeezed them tight, thinking of that moment, the Admiral's face resting in her lap, wishing she'd pushed him toward her, into the layers of toile and gauze and bunting. He would have capitulated, she knew. Anything for the voyage.

But all that was left of the Admiral was the yellow diamond ring. Like most gifts in the history of gift giving, objects whose meanings are lost on recipients, the ring had gone straight to the Symbolic Junkyard of Forsaken Gifts. The Cardinal had looked at the Admiral and the Admiral had looked at his map. Now, the ring's yellow diamonds coruscated in the thick, tropical light, tied to a string dangling from the end of a pole.

Her Highness received his first letter from the island weeks after the Admiral died, his toes cooked separate from the rest of the meal the natives discarded. The Admiral, having understood that all elements of discovery had a price tag and would save his reputation and ensure the financing of future expeditions, had marketed the place like a twenty-dollar whore. Everything was usable, sellable, smeltable, shippable, eatable, drinkable, smokable, wearable. He even claimed that the flocks of cantankerous parrots blotting out the blue of the sky were the tastiest flesh he'd ever sunk his teeth into. He yanked out their iridescent feathers and sawed off their emerald green wings, and cooked them unseasoned over a smoky fire just to prove his point. There wasn't much meat on a parrot, and the flesh was slightly bitter. "Armpit acidic" is how the Tribe Taster would have described its flavor, before he and his tribe were annihilated. Nonetheless, parrot eating was later considered the utmost in sophistication among the Spanish who built their colonial courts on the hills above the white lagoons. The aristocrats trained the parrots to hurl insults at them, and thereby a grand pantomime of insult and injury was played out, a kind of dinner theater. Parricide is murdering someone to whom you owe reverence. This was not parricide. The birds, to whom the Spanish owed nothing, spoke profanely and deserved to be punished, and their death elevated the vulgar ceremony of eating to the noble proceedings of justice.

The purest of maps is the treasure map—the essence of cartography, its ethanol. With the riches of this unexpected island mapped out, the Queen sent expedition after expedition, consoling herself by neutralizing the Admiral's memory as one name lost in a long list of explorers who curried her favor and went East. Or West, as it turned out. But the riches that scended over the waves of the Dark Ocean arrived on the Dark Continent with an unintended gift from beyond the green jungle drapery: syphilis. The Queen was its first mainland victim, but she spread it amply before expiring. In Second Empire Paris, where it was rampant, they called this disease "flâneur's curiosity." But it wasn't simply a disease, a tropical so-called malady. It was phantom testimony of the Europeans' taste for suffering, infection and luxury. The Second Empire Poet, in his rose gloves and bloody cravat, said the man unthirsty for the consolations of pockmarked, disease-ridden women was a harp with no bass string. This was a later era, when the taste for luxury, suffering and infection was better understood. The Poet himself loved pockmarked women. "I feel sorry," he said, "for the man who does not."

3

Goodbye tropical traveler! they called, waving. It was a small crowd that had accompanied her to the Lake City train platform. She lifted up her petticoats and stepped onto the scuff grate. She was light. It was the gown that was heavy. Flounces with three hundred dollars worth of gold coins sewn into the hems, like the jeweled bridal corset of a Romanov heiress. Her name was light as well: Aloha Oe. Like a shrimp chip, a tuft of cloud-pink cotton candy. A word that meant hello, and also goodbye. The people on the platform waved goodbye as the train rolled slowly east.

The idea was born in the tractor beam of a Kineto-scope, a cylinder of dusty light that splashed onto a linen screen at Lake City's newly built Palace of Moving Actualities, one of only three in the entire state of Colorado. Aloha saw bleached flickering images of the streets of Havana: black shadows on a white wall and men in rumpled duck suits and Panama hats. Then Theodore Roosevelt posing for the camera before he turned to charge up a hill. The film cut to natives working for the United Fruit Company, chomping on fibrous sugar cane and putting chilled custard apples in what seemed to be their underwear. To cool themselves while they worked, was Aloha's educated guess. She'd seen the painted transparencies of stereorama, panorama, zoopraxiscope—hardly wonders compared with the dusty, marvelous light splashing on the linen screen. It was like watching her own dreams. As if she'd dreamed about the Spanish losing the war and this dank paradise opening, the new version of the Western frontier. The distance between her and the palm shadows on a white wall, the giant stalks of bananas violently hacked from the trees and thudding to the earth, the men putting chilled custard apples in their underwear, was the distance between a place on a map and a slab of actual land, surrounded by a foamed crepe of waves. Or wood and wood grain alcohol. Things that were vastly different and yet linked. The light splashing on the screen, almost a déjà vu, tricked her into getting on a train, then another train, then a boat that floated the bluish purple gulf stream to the Caribbean.

As she stepped off the gangplank, high above the garbage-strewn harbor, her skirts tugged at her like she was wading into waist-deep water with her clothes on. The weight of the coins made it hard to walk, but it was better than gilding her teeth and pulling them out one by one with pliers like a traveling Roma. She wandered the greasy cobblestone streets amidst strange faces, humidity, sewage and factory smoke. It began pouring rain, as if all the moisture in the air had been leading to something, a necessary release. When the rain stopped, clouds wheeled out like theatre sets being replaced for the next act. Sun flooded in, virile and bright. She bought a glass of cane juice and sat on the cement benches of the Prado, under the causarina trees. Surrender yourself to the heat, she thought, her heavy skirts pulling, her dress sweat-soaked and plastered to her body. Women paraded by, their faces painted to resemble polished taffeta, streaks of creme blush glowing on their cheeks, their hair lacquered and coiled like ribbon candy into magnificent looped piles. She was watching them, these probably-prostitutes, and didn't notice the young man walking toward her, carrying a leather valise. She looked up and there he was, blue eyes that were not an innocent infant's blue, but dark as cobalt, like a shadow was passing over his face. May I sit here? he asked in a faint accent, from where she didn't know.

That's how it had started, she would later remember, when it was too late to say no, or that she was just leaving. He was too likable, too handsome, but attraction fused with trouble is a complex molecule, containing magnetic parts tempting her to find out just what kind of trouble. That she went to his rooming quarters unchaperoned didn't matter. That he made actualities that were really fictions didn't matter either—what could survive such a radical transition, from the vast unknowable world to a contained column of flickering light hitting a wall? He'd filmed the sinking of a Spanish armada in Santiago Bay. His footage was a puppet show, photographs of ships glued to paste board. The stage was his bathtub, with grains of turquoise-blue vegetable dye sifted into the water. The explosions, thimbles of gunpowder on little wooden blocks, which he detonated with alcohol-soaked cotton balls. For smoke, he blew cigar exhalations into the frame.

Ferdinand K figured she was probably not a prostitute, even if she seemed to come from nowhere, have no family, and gold coins hidden in her clothes. No one had followed them, no pimp or madam as far as he knew. A week after he found her wilting on a Prado bench, he ran out of money. She opened her hem, a savings account she withdrew with a seam-ripper. He made her a partner and changed the name of his company to Aloha Fantoscope. He and Aloha filmed more miniature sets, did things with mirrors, mirror facing mirror for a fake infinity (but what is "real infinity?" Infinity represented is still infinity). Sitting on the floor, cutting up film, they looked at each other, irises wheeling open. In between them was another infinity—the infinite distance, enacted by closeness, between two people.

In the distance between paper ships and cigar smoke, and what Ferdinand K had seen from a hill above the bay while he frantically tried to repair his camera—American marines blowing up Spanish vessels, a forty-five mile path of destruction and lakes of burning kerosene floating on the harbor—a broad space opened up, a place to maneuver with no accountability. Between battleships and sonic war and miniatures in dyed-blue bathtub water. Between bridal bed and brothel beds. The mirror of Aloha's eyes and the mirror above him on a water-stained ceiling, which he avoided by keeping his pay-pleasure missionary. And then there was his dream of projecting advertisements into the low fluffs of cloud that drifted over the city like tugboats. Aloha Fantoscope! There was the distance between it and the traceless reality of where the last of Aloha's money, generously invested in his cloud advertising scheme, had actually gone: into the childlike hands of harlots, who advertised not on clouds, but the balconies of Calle Belga. He had a weakness. Aloha's last gold piece was spent on a pockmarked girl who'd simply grabbed his arm and said you—you're coming with me. There was that joke about what a man needs to survive: food, shelter, papaya and strange papaya. In a world where papaya isn't a fruit but the damp, warm syncline between a woman's thighs.

* * *

Poor Aloha had believed him when he said the clouds above the city were like a film screen, but one that everyone could see. Penniless, she went to a bank to try to get a loan. She had nowhere to turn, and now she'd be having this child— The banker interrupted her. Why not just project your advertisements on the moon, hmm? He didn't care about her sob story or any child. It was out of his hands, he said. The banks were American-owned now, decisions were made in New York and she should ask her own government to help. What could he do, if she had no collateral, no credit, no cosigner? She left in a hormone surge, weeping.

When she'd first seen him on the Prado, Ferdinand K's cobalt eyes, twinkling and dark, had lured her to his room, unchaperoned. Now, they were turning a curdled yellow. His irises were frozen, hatches stuck in one position. Then he had oozing sores, one directly between his congealing cobalt eyes. His heart beat so violently that his fingertips pulsed in sync. A doctor came. He diagnosed the unmistakable symptoms of Flâneur's Curiosity. She paid the doctor by breastfeeding him. There was no milk yet, it was a pantomime (but a pantomime of breast suckling is breast suckling, as a picture of infinity is infinite). When she returned to the room, Ferdinand was dead.

If you're American, the banker had said to Aloha, then go to an American bank. The last Spanish dominion of the new world was supposedly erased by the war, by the end of slavery, the American marines, the newly consolidated sugar companies. But if the leaseholders were in New York, the banks themselves were Old World ornate, with silver doorknockers, gilded lobby mirrors and plush upholstery. Havana was a Paris of the Antilles, complete with colonnades, call girls, and French pornography. Gaming parlors, lobster palaces and luxury suites. The Prado was even lit by Parisian-style *papillon*, butterfly-shaped gaslights. But Paris transplanted to the tropics, with its humidity, deluges and brine, was an organ partly rejected. The scrollwork on the colonnades was crumbled and eroded by the Caribbean air sweeping through the porticoes. The glassined *voluptés bizarres* moldered on the display stands from dampness, and the butterfly lamps were caked with brine. Saltpeter turned all the doorknockers green. Silver sweated and a black lace of mold edged in around the mirrors. The plush collected bucketfuls of dust from the dense and chaotic streets. It clung to the creamy white satin and flocking in the luxury suites, turning all the walls a brick-powder pink.

People shut their windows against the pinkish dust and the incessant sound of African drumming coming from the slums. Where just-freed blacks sacrificed chickens for Our Lady of Mercy and hung *voudoun* trinkets over an iron lawn jockey with a face like their own. The prostitutes, mostly Spanish and French, were all stricken with Flâneur's Curiosity. To mask the pocks, they powdered their complexions so heavily that they all looked like spooked biscuits, ill and fanning themselves on the balconies of Calle Belga.

Aloha walked aimlessly with her K-child, in her penniless, sweat-stained clothes. She was American, but barred from entering the American Telegraph Company and wiring a message. No money, and no one to wire it to. The Americans who weren't just abstract leaseholders were mercenaries and AWOL factotums left over from the war. They lurked along the streets in their uniforms, unable to assimilate but with nowhere else to go. Farmers came into town on foot, headed for kangaroo court to lose their land to property registrars with life appointments. Across from the ports, black hustlers leaned under the colonnades in torn shirts and rope shoes, with magnificent biceps and thighs, cigarettes dangling from their purple mouths. Chinese men—the few who hadn't suicided themselves in hopes of making it back to the Orient—strolled with mulatta wives and Mongolian-looking toddlers between them.

Aloha wove amidst the black hustlers and the Chinese undead, pinkish dust in her eyes, blinking and misplaced. The only people who made sense were the melee of Spanish and local, a blend who might have fit in if it weren't for doctrines and lending notes, and the perversions of the royal decrees that had brought about their race to begin with. Everyone here was lost, wandering under the balconies where the flour-faced beauties with raking coughs and rapid heartbeats fanned themselves and said you—you're coming with me.

DEBOUCHMENT

"Our life here isn't particularly violent," the woman said, after the other woman made the comment that it was. This happened at the Pan-American club. In an era after the Spanish ate the parrots to extinction (while the natives stuck to grilled banana heart), and before the Russians came, with their Brutalist architecture and their smoked pig's fat.

"I'm not saying there isn't violence," the woman continued. "But viol*ence* and viol*ent* are different. It's the difference between incident and intent." Some features of this in-between time, at the Pan-American club: Black Forest-style castles in sugar cane fields, saltwater swimming pools reflecting tessellated rectangles of sunlight. And cinema palaces with love seats in the back row.

Although there was the plantation boss, she remembered. A very decent man, really, even if it's true there was a killing connected to him. It seems he had done it, she remembered, that was the connection. But that was in Louisiana and a long time ago. Mr. Flamm, the paymaster, was killed, true enough. But that was the blacks, and their love of chopping people up with those horrific machetes they carry around. They really do look like savages and it's the strangest thing to hear them speaking French—

Also in this in-between era, after the Spanish, who cooked their parrots so slowly they remained alive as they were removed from the oven, and before the Russians, who took the scrubbers off the chimneys and let the red dust rain down: a dictator's estate, with artificial waterfall and presidential barbershop, a divorcée's mausoleum, with amber Lalique windows, and the addition of cheval-de-frise on the low walls of Spanish colonial buildings, to prevent vagrants from sitting.

Those who hadn't gone to the Pan-American club were at home listening to the faith healer on the radio. His was the only program, this time of night. Unless you wanted to listen to the bandits illegally broadcasting from their camp in the mountains. Bearded ruffians instructing people to burn sugar cane, to tie a kerosene-soaked rag to the tail of a rat and set him loose in the cane break.

Also in this in-between era, before the Russians and their Brutalist apartments, and after the parrots, who looked up from the dinner plates as their wings were sawed off with serrated knives: a supply of what are called black pineapple grenades—philological proof of destruction's commitment to the Tropics.

The woman had said loudly, for everyone in the club to hear, that she was sick of all the violence. *"To here,"* she'd slurred, and put her hand up to her neck. She was drunk, as everyone was, most of the time. She was not a person to be taken seriously. The type of woman who bleaches her hair and then dyes it dark again, in order to get that coarse, ratted, bedroom effect. After she said it she started an argument with her husband. Some women are very skilled at that. As soon as he started to fight back, she dropped her drink on the marble floor as a diversion.

A constant in all three eras: syphilis, tobacco, and trees with fruit whose flesh is the pink of healthy mucus membranes. A fruit that smells like women's shampoo.

"Put a glass on the radio and my voice will serenade it," the faith healer told listeners. Those who were lucky enough to go to the studio had their water serenaded with his flashlight beam. "Buy lottery tickets with numbers ending in six. In four. In zero ... Drink the agua serenada before you go to sleep." It was a procedure for winning the lottery. The week before, the finance minister had won the lottery, and used the money to buy a house in West Palm Beach. It seemed he expected to be relocating sometime soon.

This was Christmastime, and there were humans hanging in the trees beyond the security fence. She herself had a cheerful breadfruit sapling in the living room—the refrigerated shipment of Douglas fir had not been able to get through because the bandits had blocked the roads eastward. She hung the breadfruit tree with strings of tiny lights and hollow metallic balls, and sang Jungle Bells and other carols with the children.

Local fragrances, in addition to the flesh-pink shampoo fruit: the feminine traces that lingered in the powder room of the Pan-American club (Arpège, Fibah, and boredom), and the fetid jungle breath beyond the club's meticulous gardens (rot, rot, and rot).

Like the bandits, the faith healer had to broadcast illegally. He had been condemned by the State, which accused him of feeding listeners fake hope. Passive hope, like baby food, like liquor, a set of baroque and empty promises. They didn't realize he was working for them, in their favor. "All problems have a solution," the faith healer said. "We all have a right to succeed in business, in study, in sports, in gambling, in love." There were new laws. Palm readers, hypnotists and self-appointed gurus were all convicted. Also, vendors who sold magic powders, aphrodisiacs and remedies by mail. The state banned broadcasts on divination and the interpretation of dreams, on anything that stimulated beliefs opposed to civilization, under a federal sub-clause called "crimes of passion." Only the lottery numbers were okay.

The woman who dropped her drink had calmed down. She said to her husband in a defeated voice, "I wish everybody would just be quiet. It's too much. All this talk of phosphorus and ammonia. I can't keep it straight— what we have, what they have. I'm not a goddamned chemist." Her husband was scooping up the remains of her drink, which was now just the base of a glass, surrounded by cheval-de-frise.

"Those who wrong me will meet grave misfortune," the faith healer announced on his illegal broadcast.

"*They've* got the phosphorus," her husband said. "And *we've* got the ammonia."

"But what the hell does it matter?" she asked.

"Because phosphorus is a weapon. They drop it from planes." He set the remains of her broken glass on the bar, gesturing to the bartender to make her a new one. "And ammonia is a target. Those tanks next to the nickel factory across the channel—they'll explode."

"I know God's deepest secrets," the faith healer said. He was not a religious man.

The chandeliers swung, in the rooms where the ceilings hadn't simply vaulted and then collapsed. There was a rip of pops from somewhere inside. Women who had been in the powder room when the explosion occurred reeled straight into the enormous mirrors that were mounted on the walls of the powder room lounge. In their disoriented panic, they mistook the silvered glass for open space. (Euclid still applied, if not to history, to at least the layout of the Pan-American club). The mirrors crashed to the floor. The women wandered aimlessly, sliced up, blood batiking their faces. "It's broken," one of them said, holding her hands over her nose, which flumed garnet down to her chin. The first woman in this story was found wandering in the foyer, glass crunching under her heels. There was music in her head, jangly and instrumental, with a high-pitched and chimy af-ter-trace. Music you'd pump out of a hand-crank organ, she thought to herself, but pictured no monkey. The monkeys here didn't work—they hung from their cages, blinking at you with their moist, human eyes. The music was getting louder, more high-pitched around the edges. Blood flooded her vision. She said, "Can someone please turn that down?" She said it as loud as she could, but the music drowned her out.

THE STRANGE CASE
OF RACHEL K

The blue lights flipped on. Smoky haze drifted above the tables.

"Introducing, from Paris, zazou dancer Rachel K!"

The marquee said Rachel K, *French Variety Dancer*, but the French Nazi had known immediately she wasn't French. Whatever she was or wasn't, she looked like a liar and he liked liars. He imagined there was someone for whom honesty was a potent seduction, but the French Nazi was not that sentimental someone. Seduction, he knew, was a slew of projections, disguises, denials. What could you claim to accurately know about anyone, much less a stranger to whom you were attracted? And yet you could claim, accurately, that a person was evasive, and that their evasions interested you.

He'd watched her show several nights in the Cabaret Tokio's Pam-Pam Room, when he finally decided to break the wax seal on their silent conversation of glances. He stared coolly, continuously, wearing a colonial dictator's eyeglasses, with heavy tortoiseshell frames and aubergine-tinted lenses. In her cycle of periodically eyeing him, Rachel K was eventually forced to meet his gaze. He nodded almost imperceptibly. She came toward him and plopped onto his lap like a child.

"Are you an ambassador or something?" she asked. She thought his suit looked expensive. His crisp, white shirt cuffs seemed somehow dignitary-quality.

The French Nazi said yes, exactly, an ambassador, but they both knew it was a lie. That ambassador was a code for something complex and possibly unspeakable, a word they both saw with quotes around it. Rachel K was wearing black fishnet stockings. He could see their pattern, even in the dim blue light. He liked the diaphanous allure of fishnets. They were an enticement in the guise of a barrier, like a beaded curtain hung over a doorway says "come in," not "stay out," its beads telegraphing that what's inside is enchanted and special. He put his hand on her knee. Her skin felt slightly cool, bare and smooth. He ran his finger up the inside of her thigh carefully, as though drawing a line on dew-frosted glass, leaving a skin-toned smear in the cross-hook pattern of her fishnets.

"An illusion, a painting," he said, and looked at her with a bemused smile.

He had a vague memory of Parisian women wearing paint-on stockings during the war. But that was all over. This was 1952. The girl had made her own perverse style out of scarcity, and he was impressed. And what was supposed to be an enticement, a fine membrane of netting that begged not just "'remove me" but "rip me to shreds" could not be ripped to shreds. It could be removed, of course, with water and soap, but such a ritual without the purpose of gaining sexual access, would have no meaning. Why bother, when he could have her as she was? Her stockings were as material as the sun-shadow of chain-link on a prison wall. He thought of Inge, the German girl with whom he'd toured the Rhineland before enlisting in the Charlemagne Division. Little Inge who insisted he tear through her intricate cat's cradle of garters and stays, girdle, corset and underwear. He would burst through snaps and panels, and tug tight-fitting elasticized garments down around the German girl's knees, dismantling underwear fortifications in order to penetrate the frontier of her pretend-virginity. Sometimes he became impatient, pried his hand into her underwear and simply jerked the crotch panel to the inside of her thigh, to clear the way. The tearing sound of unforgiving fabric would cause Inge to let out a little moan, as if the fabric itself were the delicate folds of her innocence. With paint-on stockings, there was nothing to burst through. No garters, stays, or snaps. Only flesh.

Rachel K nodded yes, that she'd painted them on. "They were perfect too—until you marked me," She extended her legs to survey her work. "They took me all day to finish." She'd used a sable cosmetic brush and a pot of liquid mascara, drawing lines that crossed at angles to make diamonds, her foot lodged on the windowsill of her kitchenette. Like prayer, it was a quiet, obliterative meditation that opened up an empty space in her thoughts, a not-her. But it wasn't prayer, and she wanted the space of not-her to remain empty, rather than fill with the presence of god.

"You spent an entire day painting your legs?" he asked.

"Some girls spend hours plucking their eyebrows," she said. "Burning sugar cubes and dropping them in absinthe."

He nodded. "And you do this instead."

"I do lots of things."

"I'm sure you do," he said. "It does say 'variety' dancer, after all. *French* variety dancer, no less." It was a style of flirting, exposing her fabrications to provoke her into new ones.

"Maybe my dance is French-*style*," she said. "But it's more than that. My grandfather, Ferdinand K, was French. He came to Cuba to film the Spanish-American war." Her grandfather, Ferdinand K, had gone east to film not the war but the hardwood fires. Forests of campeachy, purpleheart and mahogany that had been burned to make way for sugar cane, fires so magnificent and hot they cracked his camera lens. He'd decided it was safer to stay in Havana and construct dioramic magic tricks. And so he blew up the USS Maine in a hotel sink with Chinese firecrackers and then sold the reels as war footage.

The French Nazi examined her in the dim blue light. She had a narrow face, dark eyes, the full lips and large teeth of a Manouche gypsy or German Jew. "K could be a number of things, mademoiselle," he said, stroking her cheek with the back of his hand. "But K is not French."

"They said he was French."

51

"They?"

"Actually, my mother."

"And she was—"

"A nothing. A stranger who left me here when I was thirteen." She and her mother had ducked into the Tokio from the blinding sun of midday Havana. It was so dark inside the club that Rachel K could barely see. They waited at the Pam-Pam Room bar until a manager appeared from a back office, trailing Cigar smoke. He breathed audibly and in his labored breath she understood that he'd taken her on. That was ten years ago. She'd been at the Tokio so long now that it was a kind of mother. It gave her life a shape. Other girls passed through, regarded cabaret dancing as momentary and sordid, always hoping for some politician or businessman to rescue them. Because the Tokio gave her life a shape and never sent her fretting over imagined alternatives, Rachel K was free in a way the other girls weren't. She had longings as well, but they weren't an illness to be cured. They were part of who she was, and it was these very longings that reinforced the deeper reconciliation to her situation.

The French Nazi said thirteen seemed rather young for a debut in her line of work. Not in the tropics, Rachel K replied, where girls reach puberty at ten. She told him how the Tokio dressing room attendants had draped her in spangles, pompoms, and gold sartouche trim. They were kind, middle-aged women with smoky voices and thick masks of makeup. They'd crimped her locks and painted her mouth in lipstick imported from Paris, a reddish-black like blood gone dark from asphyxiation. Covered her breasts with tasseled pasties and put her onstage in the Pam-Pam Room. Voilà. Here she was.

Sometimes it seemed that her entire adolescence had been lived in the dressing room mirrors of the Caba-ret Tokio. She'd spent hours gazing into them, locked out and wanting to get inside, where the world was the same, but silvery and greenish, doubled and reversed. The same, but different. When she was alone in the dressing room she'd sidle up and press her cheek to the silver and look sidelong into the mirror, hoping to catch a glimpse—of what?—whatever its invisible secret was. She had faith that there was some secret at the heart of the invisibility, even if faith meant allowing for the pos-sibility that there was no secret, that invisibility had no heart. If she knew the mirror's secret, she'd know how to pass through to the other side. To a greenish-silver province that was her world, but reversed.

Now, it occurred to her that she never looked at mirrors

as mystery spaces anymore. Maybe she'd passed through without knowing it.

"From Paris, zazou dancer Rachel K!" the announcer calls into the microphone.

There's a clatter of applause.

The French Nazi remembers zazou. It was a jazz thing during the war. Girls in chunky heels and fishnets, with dark lipstick and parasols. Or maybe it was berets, he can't recall. Boys in zoot suits, an unseemly glisten of salad oil in their hair. They were bohemians who struck poses near the outdoor tables at Café de Flore, bumming cigarettes and slurping whatever broth you left in the bottom of your soup bowl. It wasn't about poverty. It was a style of dissidence. By the time the zazou were being rounded up by German patrols, he was far away from Paris. Marching waist-deep into a cold apocalypse with a Panzerfaust over his shoulder.

The accompanist touches a few keys on the piano, the beginning of an old-fashioned danzón. Rachel K floats out from behind a Chinoiserie screen, draped in black chiffon and a cascade of rooster tail feathers that glint metallic green under the lights. The partition and a satin chaise longue transform the stage into a girl's private dressing room, a feminine alcove of upholstery, unrobing and mirrors with an audience of men watching intently as she drops her feathers and chiffon on the chaise, and steps forward. A tropical wraith with chemical blonde hair. Blue lights illuminate her white skin, white like a body filmed underwater. A body glimpsed across a night-lit swimming pool, or in the glaucous depths of dreams.

The "variety" of her dance comes after the show: discreet hotel room trysts, unlike the blatant commerce that goes on everywhere in Havana, at all times of day, behind bed sheets strung across vacant lots. She eludes the term "whore" with the smoke and mirrors of "demi-mondaine." Girl of the underworld, an in-between space, a twilight, neither light nor dark, but a shimmering, aqueous blue. She makes a life out of twilight.

Even in her real privacy, in her dressing room or in her alcove apartment, she is never purely alone, but playing the part of alone for some invisible watcher. Her stage partition and parasol are even the same Chinoiserie print, so that walking to buy cigarettes or milk she can't escape the feeling of standing onstage, dropping the green-glinting feathers in a fluffy pile, a loose feather or two detaching to float by itself. The boundary between her private life and public life has blurred, as has the boundary between engaging her body only in intimate pleasures with people she trusts, and using it as an object she owns. She suspects these boundaries are delicate and probably can't be repaired. But this is on some level a relief, to a girl who believes only in the present, and certainly not in guilt. There's no use in fretting, or attempting to fix what cannot be.

She often went to the Hotel Nacional, to suites flocked in satiny white, with dictators, diplomats, Americans, and on one occasion Havana's Cadillac dealer, Amadeo Barletta Barletta, an Italian even shorter than she was, with burning eyes, ravaged skin, and currency so freshly minted it seemed like game-board money.

It was in one of these satin-flocked suites that the French Nazi stayed. This Frenchman, a certain Christian de la Mazière—aristocratic playboy, memoirist, ex-Charlemagne Division Waffen SS—took a jetliner from Paris to Havana and then a limousine from the airport. He bubble-bathed in the sunken marble tub at his suite in the Hotel Nacional. Ordered a split of Perri-er-Jouet, two boiled eggs and a saltshaker. Ate his light lunch and then headed for the Cabaret Tokio. He sat at a table in the back of the Pam-Pam Room watching Rachel K dance, her golden sartouche whipping like a lasso as she swung around a pole, no less graceful than a ballerina. But ballet dancers were like porcelain figu-rines, elegantly molded and coldly unsexed. Rachel K was warm soft-contoured flesh. With a gaudily feminine spill of platinum curls, and those barely bobbing firm-jelly breasts that are not only rare, a happy coincidence of genetics and miracles, but utterly time-sensitive, existing only in a slim window of youth. She spun her tassels left and then right, then one left and one right, miniature roulette wheels swirling in two directions. De la Mazière watched her kneel before the blue lights and smile coyly with her plump Manouche or German Jewish mouth for the men at the front tables. They were serious and stoic, and he understood that the cabaret was their church. Her show, an engrossing sermon they took in with naive and absolute faith. He was serious too, but while the other men watched her with awe—an exotic creature as mysterious as conical rays of divine light coming through a stained-glass window—he'd immediately seen something he was sure they could not. She'd gauzed her person in persona, but as she jiggled her body in the blue light, he sensed the person slipping through, person and persona in a kind of elaborate tangle. With her French theme, her mannered charm, he detected a creature whose mode was duplicity. He knew this mode. It was his own.

He studied her firm-jelly breasts, the silver sequins of her G-string, and her blue-pale skin with a kind of detached desire, in no hurry to get closer. He was patient, almost perversely so: The delay of pleasure was its own special and more refined category of pleasure. He didn't offer to buy her a drink after her show. Didn't even let her catch him staring. He began going to the Tokio nightly, showing up just as it was her turn to dance. He sat in a shadowy back corner of the Pam-Pam Room, where the tables were always empty, and where he had a clear view of the stage, as well as the hallway that led to the curtained private booths. He enjoyed watching drunk and enthusiastic businessmen clumsily swat the booth curtains out of their way, duck in with girls who wore sly, proud looks on their faces. The men and the girls each thinking it was they who'd triumphed over the other. He watched the Tokio bartender, a man with down-turned eyes that made his face melancholy, like a song in a minor key, as the bartender played canasta with two bored and customerless dancers, girls whom de la Mazière guessed had no choice but to bide their time, waiting for specialty clientele. One was much too thin, with an unappealing, shovel-like pelvis. The other, maximally fleshy and pushing six-feet, a regular giantess. After watching the giantess lose at canasta and then circulate the room twice, approaching him on both sweeps, he dug out a couple of pesos for a lap dance. He suspected Rachel K might notice he'd bought company, but that was all part of the game. Because what he waited for felt inevitable, he could sample a giantess, get her squirming and giggling and moving her brown Caribbean hips in just the right way, and do it with full concentration.

"From Paris!"

Rachel K steps out. Opening notes float from the piano. The blue lights are angled toward her, mounted on the lip of the stage, and in them she can see mostly a screen of curling smoke, and through the smoky screen, the men in the front two or three rows. The lights block her view of those in the back but those in the back don't matter. The men near the stage lay down bills, and it's for them that she dances.

She drops her feather boa on the chaise. Feathers that are cheaply dyed, and stain her fingers and the back of her neck a faint corpse-gray.

"Zazou dancer Rachel K!"

If she says she's from Paris, she's from Paris, is her sentiment. Being from Paris means filing her nails to a point and lacquering them in Hemorrhage Red. Drinking beer with grenadine. Carrying a parasol made of rice paper, with a Chinoiserie pattern like her stage partition—a peacock, lotus and reeds. Wearing painted-on fishnets, dressing like a zazou in short skirts and stacked wooden heels. Eating mouthfuls of cocaine. Douching with champagne. She believes that people are born every minute of their lives, and what they are in each of those minutes is what they are completely. Zazou, and from Paris, are things she does. Things she is by virtue of doing them.

An executive of the United Fruit Company, a Mr. something Stites—she couldn't remember his first name and simply called him "you"—took her east to Oriente in his private plane. She'd been hesitant to go. He seemed like a person who was dangerous because he didn't know which parts of him were rotten, or even that he harbored rot. "All this belongs to us," he said, as they hedgehopped over green cane fields. "Three hundred thousand acres. Those are our boats, anchored off shore there. You see them?" Maybe he wasn't dangerous after all, she decided. He simply wanted a showgirl to marvel over his sugar empire. They landed at company headquarters and she ran through a canopy of banana groves near the airport, trees with long, flat leaves, taller than she was and loaded with dank and heavy clusters of bananas, a strange purple flower dangling off the end of each cluster. She put her hand around a banana stalk. "They're full of water, pure water," the executive said. It felt like a chilled human limb with a cold pulse.

The girls had mostly left de la Mazière to himself at his lone back table, having pegged him as quirky, disinterested, and cheap. Until he got the giantess gyrating on his lap. The next evening, girls began fluttering around him. They thought he was German and kept saying, "Das ist gut, ja? Das ist gut?" De la Mazière nodded distractedly, smiled and said "Ja, gut" in his French accent. He ordered a rum drink with crushed mint and morphine crystals dissolving in a slush of ice. Sipped his drink and stole looks at Rachel K, whose white body moved past his table, her little-girl hand in the grip of some high-level politician's. A Latin tomcat, foppish, with his white dinner jacket, his combed and polished mustache, a wristwatch whose diamonds caught the club lights and sent out angled glints. The politician had been standing in a half-circle of bodyguards, checking his watch. Waiting, as it turned out, for Rachel K. She and the politician—the president, de la Mazière later realized—disappeared into one of the special curtained booths off the Pam-Pam Room. De la Mazière distracted himself by ordering another drink. He tickled the girl on his lap, who erupted in giggles. She straddled him. Took his tinted dictator's glasses and tried them on. Placed her hand on the crotch of this French SS officer—memoirist, minor aristocrat, dreamer of extremes. "Das ist gut?" she asked, smiling, pressing with her hand, his tinted glasses slipping down her nose. "Ja," he replied, "gut."

Marcel bequeathed his aunt Leonie's couch to a bordello, and whenever he visited the place, to tease Rachel of my Lord (but never buy her services), it unnerved him to see tarts flopped on its pink crushed velvet cushions, even if there was maybe nothing more perfect and appropriate than pink velvet plush flattening under a whore's ass. De la Mazière was different. It didn't matter to him whether he reclined on plush furniture in the lobby of the Ritz or in a squalid St. Denis cathouse. Ate his steak at Maxim's or at a colonial outpost in Djibouti, a backwater of salt factories and scorching temperatures on the bacterial mouth of the Red Sea. Properly seared steak is everywhere the same. A traitor satisfies his tastes, gets his high- and his low-grade pleasures wherever he can. In Havana, de la Mazière found occupied Paris all over again. Amidst its nude and adorned girls, morphine slushees and luxury hotel suites, he sensed a vague but unshakeable dread darkening the reverie and lawlessness. Despite the city's obvious, surreal wealth, he sniffed wretched poverty. Tall and neon-pulsing casinos staking the heart of a metropolis ringed in desperation: miles and miles of neighborhoods with no electricity, no running water, and smokily typhoid trash fires. It was occupied Paris, with Americans in Cadillacs instead of Germans in Mercedes. A sultrier climate and starrier nights, purple-mouthed girls, a cinema palace with a retractable roof. They even had Obelisk and Olympia books on Calle Belga, and obsolete French pornography—not sequestered in L'Enfer, on the top floor of the Bibliothèque Nationale, but displayed at the bookstalls, their pages riffling in the damp ocean breeze.

And there was this girl, with the face of a Manouche Gypsy or German Jew. Like a drug that binds to what's already in the wiring, she seemed formed from his own memories and longings. And yet unknowable—a cipher in pasties, painted like a doll.

Rachel K was leading President Prio, "Handsome," she called him, as if it were his name, through the Pam-Pam Room to his own VIP booth. He was not, in truth, so handsome, but he was president and vain. She and Handsome passed the mysterious Frenchman's table. A Frenchman who might have been, in fact, quite handsome. He seemed confident, amused, self-contained. A perfect loner. He'd been coming back, and each evening he was there, his presence distracted her, like he knew that she knew that he was watching her, though pretending not to, and his gaze colored her every movement. Just walking through the room, she was performing for an audience of one attentive Frenchman. It was strange, like he was whispering something and she could hear it even if she couldn't translate into language what he said. She sensed a tacit agreement between them, that they would continue for some time with this ritual of him watching her and pretending not to, whispering a silent message more voluminous, airy and complex than language could transmit. She felt sure it was better to draw out the spell than risk breaking it prematurely. And anyway, she was with Handsome, her favorite of the revolving door of presidents. They sat together in a private booth, and he gave her an opal pendant and a silk dress with a secret pocket. She kissed his mustache and let him practice his soliloquies on her.

President Prio liked to have a good time. He was a man of low ambition and lofty ideals. The press ridiculed him for his expensive and ribald tastes: caviar, Russian vodka, and fourteen-carat toilet flush handles. Photos had been leaked of him and his brother Tony jumping over the lime-upholstered sofas in the Green Room of the president's palace, in pursuit of young girls clad in short-shorts. The accompanying newspaper article told of his notorious white parties. Prio was demoralized, humiliated, persona non grata with even his own cabinet ministers. A popular radio personality, Popo de la Cruz, ranted night after night about Prio's corruption and vanity, so that people wouldn't forget. Tony moved to Venezuela and started a construction firm. Prio only went out in dark sunglasses, flanked by bodyguards. His wife wore a black illusion veil, had them sewn to the inside of all her pillbox hats. The two of them and the children got in and out of polished Buick limousines as quickly as they could, turning away from the photographer's flash.

"How about a walk. An ice cream cone?" Prio said to Rachel K, the evening he gave her the pendant and the dress. They were sitting in Prio's private booth, decorated like a Roman grotto with panorama-print Classical scenery, plaster figurines, and purple-leafed wandering Jew tumbling down the walls like ivy.

She hadn't expected a walk, an ice cream. She's expected, *Go to the palace Green Room and cooperate fully.* But his

tenderness—opals, dresses, ice cream cones—was part of
why she liked him best. Not because he spoiled her, but
because he could be embarrassing and sentimental.

They left the club and went to nearby La Rampa, a
grand avenue of deluxe sundae parlors where the rich
strolled and licked. Exclusive confection boutiques that
would later be replaced by an enormous State-run ice
cream emporium, a concrete spaceship that gave away
twenty-five thousand bowls of government-issue vanilla
and strawberry every day. A drab and massive enterprise
that would be the future government's elaborate fuck
you to the rich, to the presidents and their prostitutes,
who'd strolled and licked along La Rampa in Havana's
diamond days.

Prio chose chocolate chip and she guava, a fruit that
tasted deliciously unnatural. More like perfume than
something you were supposed to eat. They were strolling and licking and window-shopping along La Rampa,
Rachel K laughing at Prio, who looked unpresidential,
she said, with ice cream in his mustache. A member of
his dark-suited security team, who normally walked a
few paces behind, approached and tapped Prio's shoulder. The man leaned in and whispered something. Prio,

still with ice cream frosting the tines of his mustache, blanched. He turned to Rachel K. "I must leave you now," he said in a shaky voice. "Lelo here will take you back to the club."

That night of strolling and licking on La Rampa was Prio's last night as president. With the military's cooperation, an army general named Batista staged a coup. "Easy as ordering a birthday cake from Schrafft's," Rachel K heard an American at the Tokio remark. One moment, Prio was on La Rampa, laughing and window-shopping, while his wife and children slept in their cream-colored sleigh beds. And then suddenly he and his family were huddling in the piss elegance of the Dominican embassy, booking airline tickets out. Batista had telephoned from Miami, promising to buy all the army officers new uniforms, and in return they gave undying loyalty. Surrounded the palace with tanks. People talked about the coup as the end of so-called democracy. Until later in the week, when the American ambassador endorsed the new government, celebrating Batista as business-friendly and a hallmark of a new era in Cuban-American relations. Prio settled in Miami and pursued a career as a stage actor. He might have been relieved, as Rachel K suspected, to have the presidency stolen from him and to pursue his long-held dream of becoming a stage actor. She herself didn't care about politics. Though on a personal level she preferred Prio to the new president, a greedy man who knew how to manipulate people but never had anything interesting to say.

De la Mazière was at his table in the back, watching the bartender with the face in a minor key play canasta with a dancer. The bartender won, but his face remained dolorous, as if winning were a burden, one more sad duty to perform. This was a few days after the coup. De la Mazière wondered about Rachel K, who she'd visit with now that Prio had fled the island. His pick would not have been a small-time gangster-leftist and his younger brother. These two entered the club and waited by the bar, awkwardly, as if they'd never been inside a place like the Tokio. Rachel K led the gangster and his brother to a booth in the back of the room. This gangster was increasingly well known. An instant enemy of the new State, he'd fired his gun on the plaza of the university in protest of the coup. The police had fired back, and then Batista shut the campus down. The younger brother had his notoriety as well, if in a different way: he was queer as a three-dollar bill, with hair on his upper lip so pre-pubescent it looked like cupcake crumbs. The three of them stayed in the booth for what seemed to de la Mazière like quite a while. When the curtain finally opened, he watched them file out. The gangster and his brother each shook Rachel K's hand, as if one of them had just sold the other a used car, or a piece of real estate. Formal handshakes among a gangster, faggot, and a variety dancer. It was certainly peculiar.

The next evening de la Mazière was watching television in his hotel suite, as Batista made his acceptance speech. He was a mulatto with soft features, a faint severity straining his smile, a mean streak that couldn't quite be suppressed. His general's uniform was littered with medals and badges, every color of stripe and ribbon. He looked ridiculous. De la Mazière thought of Darnand with his French decorations—"bonbons"—attached to his new Sturmbannführer's uniform. Medals Darnand had won fighting the Germans on the Maginot Line, pinned under his new silver-stitched SS insignia.

Batista smiled and made his face handsome. "I am a dictator with the people," he said. The television cut to footage from the day before, this Cuban army general stepping off a plane from Miami and kneeling to kiss the tarmac, apparently overcome with love for his country. Home after his exile. Prio now in exile. The army general home. Everyone switching places as the chips fell. Darnand fled to Germany, but the stakes were so much higher. He wasn't a small-time factotum from a banana republic, and there wasn't any Miami, a place to cool his heels and wait things out playing canasta under a lanai. Darnand was captured. Brought to Paris. Executed.

A memory bloomed in de la Mazière's mind of the earlier, glory days in Paris. Armistice follies and occupation fun. Civilian elites like himself, bourgeoisie, scum and profiteers roaming with pockets full of cash. The particular, hushed feeling of the city at dusk, the violet-blushing emptiness of the Parisian sky. Riding through the streets in a black Mercedes while destitute people traveled on foot, begging and scavenging. What had he cared the city was "annexed?" Or that Hitler, "le grand Jules" they called him, surveyed the Champs-Elysèes and visited Sacré-Coeur? It was a free-for-all, the old social distinctions collapsed, a place now structured less on class and more on cleverness, the gray market, the black market, privilege and opportunism. Controlled by profiteers, royalists and moneyed riffraff. Le Boeuf sur le Toit and Maxim's did booming business, packed for all-night parties of crystal-clinking pandemonium. German boys loitering in the lobby of the Ritz, their muscles pressing up against the perfectly creased fabric of their uniforms, anxious to polish your boots. Their sergeants, stripped to the waist, sun-tanned on the steps of the Louvre. At Fifine's on the Rue St. Denis, girls rode topless on carousel horses like lithe, buttery-bodied centaurs, the carousel revolving at an erotic, slow keel. An impossible time, that time in Paris. Impossible even as it was happening.

But he didn't want to return to those days, just certain parts of them. He didn't want to wait for hours at the Vichy palace while Pétain refused to see him, de la Mazière standing at attention, a Frenchman in a German uniform. And though he'd won a frozen meat medal, he'd as soon eat actual frozen meat than fight Bolsheviks again, in the heavy snows of Pomerania. A place of misery and death, where his regiment was pulverized and scattered and he became an animal, eating raw horseflesh and sleeping in the snow. He understood painfully well that you couldn't recreate a moment of ignorance, a luminous bubble winking in the folds of memory. A bubble that he later

72

saw had floated in a tide of darkness. All he could do was keep going until he found a bubble somewhere on the map. In Havana there was no war, no snow, no shame. There was, instead, softness, flesh and decadence masking some kind of horror, like makeup over a bruise.

Earlier on the evening that de la Mazière and Rachel K finally spoke, she'd been entertaining Batista. Batista in his medal-glittering uniform, a dictator wonderfully "with" the people. De la Mazière had watched as she and the president, surrounded by thugs, passed through the Pam-Pam Room to a VIP grotto.

"You have friends in high places," de la Mazière said to her.

"Who says they're friends?" she asked.

"Ah. How right you are. Friendship is built on loyalty," he said. "Not services rendered by a *fille de joie*. But you and the former president, Prio, I think you were friendly."

"Friendliness is a service," she said. "He's gone, and I'm not hearing any violins."

De la Mazière smiled. "You're too busy cavorting with his enemy." He had his two hands clasped around her upper thigh, a garter belt of human fingers banding her leg. "If this was Paris, after the—" he paused and made quotes with his fingers, "—'liberation'—they'd shave your head, mademoiselle." He reached up and stroked her coarse blonde hair with the attention of a hairdresser assessing locks he was about to shear.

The French women who'd cavorted with Germans couldn't hide their Nazi trysts any better than their ears, while de la Mazière wove incredible fabrications and repatriated with little problem. Spent his jail time in a luxury cell, his labor assignment: organizing the warden's formal dinner parties. Until a mysterious yellow telex arrived, pardoning him after only five years. Returning to France had been in a sense the same as leaving to fight against it: both were thresholds of radical disconnection. Twice now, he'd burned all his papers and identification. Twice, crossing a threshold had promised an instant crumbling of his own past.

The Frenchman was grabbing locks of Rachel K's hair and running them through his fingers. He pulled firmly at her scalp, but it was a pleasant sort of firmly, a gently-firmly.

Friendliness is a service," he said. "Of course. You need privacy. Ease of mobility. People get in the way."

They really did, she thought. Even Prio. Near the end, he came around too frequently, and she felt a wearying duty to keep fixing herself into something familiar and consistent that he could recognize.

"Friendship," de la Mazière said, tugging her hair to angle her face toward his, "is a barbaric concept."

He was looking at her, and she had the funny feeling that if time and everyone suspended in its viscous grip was just then frozen, only the two of them would be left as they were, sentient and unfrozen.

"It's funny, I must have been mistaken," he said. "I remembered your hair as quite a bit longer. Even last night." It was above her neck. He knew he wasn't mistaken. He was being coy.

"I cut it," she said. "Bleached hair doesn't have full value." But the truth was that she'd overvalued her hair. In every fantasy she had, every impossible scenario that floated into her mind, she always had waist-length hair. As if long hair were part of a tendency to indulgence, delusion, impossibility. And so she'd bladed it to her chin that morning, long platinum hair gone into the trash. Slumped and lustrous, like a discarded wig.

"What do you like to do?" he asked, "besides cut your hair and paint your legs?"

All men at the Tokio asked this. *What do you like?* It was part of the tête-à-tête of her profession, but what the men wanted was a limited variety of set responses: *I like pleasing you. I like squirming on your lap. I like to fantasize about a man just like you watching me take my clothes off. I think about it when I'm alone, and I have to put my own little girl hands in my underwear, just to stop the longing to be on your lap.* Gullibility was beside the point: hearing these things was a performance the men were paying for. They didn't really want to know what she liked, and it never would have occurred to her to tell them. But she figured that the Frenchman, with his bemused half-smile, was too clever to want such an obvious put-on. He seemed to understand flirtation— real flirtation, and not a bluntly performed simulation of it. She suspected that if she said "I like squirming on your lap," he'd surely laugh his head off, and at her expense.

"I like those few days of the year when it's cold here, at the end of hurricane season," she said. "It's cold enough you need a sweater. And at night, blankets. But I don't fall asleep with blankets over me. I leave them down at the end of the bed and make myself fall asleep uncovered. When I wake up later in the night, freezing cold, I reach down and pull up all the blankets."

De la Mazière thought of this girl making herself fall

76

asleep cold, naked and uncovered in order to then feel warmth with more intensity. He couldn't help but imagine being the warm body that smothered this petite girl, cold and shivering on a mattress. Though he didn't want to be just the warmth, he realized, but the cold as well. What preceded, in this fantasy, was him stripping the bed and leaving her shivering in nothing. Maybe underwear. Him, making her cold. And then warm.

He looked at her Manouche gypsy or German Jewish face, this girl with her ink-laced legs and her K name, so obviously middle European. Among giant-sized strippers, tomcat actor-presidents, gangsters and homosexuals. Still, she stuck out.

"I think you should tell me your story," he said, Not that he didn't believe the orphaned-at-a-burlesque club tale, but he wanted something else. He wasn't sure whether he wanted a made-up story or a true story, or even what the difference was. People talked about character, a defining sort of substance. But deception was a substance as well, as relevant and admirable as what it covered. If it covered anything, that is. He had great empathy for affects and evasions.

"Okay here's a story," she said. "A man named Ferdinand K came over from France. He worked in cinema.

Met a girl named Aloha. My grandmother. She was young. Younger than I am. They had a baby—my mother—the nothing, and then they both dropped dead of venereal diseases. My mother, the orphan, was a street urchin. I don't know who my father is. I told you the rest of it already."

"You've told me circumstances. Not story."

She looked slightly hurt. "Okay, fine. Maybe you should tell me *your* story," she said, catching his eye through the tinted lenses, "*Ambassador.*"

He smiled as if to say, no problem, watch me give you nothing. "I'm Christian de la Mazière. And okay, I'm not an ambassador." He paused. "I'm a journalist."

"You're lying," she said.

"I suppose I am."

"And you know what else? I have a feeling you dismiss lowly 'circumstances' because you're not willing to cough them up."

"Why should I divulge what is meaningless?" he said. "A banal dossier of 'this was my grandfather, I was steered into this or that profession.' My existence is free of those tedious things."

"I bet the opposite is true," she said. "I bet you live in a prison of your 'tedious' past."

"It isn't a prison," he said. "You'll see." And then he fell quiet, as if her accusation had sent him drifting into contemplation.

If only it were tedious, he thought at her, but didn't say out loud. *If only.* In fact, it's sordid and remarkable to have been an incidental SS. With no war, no army, no country. Only floating memories of medals and Maxim's and going to fight the Bolsheviks, thinking fascism was better than Stalin and that I was fighting for heritage and class, and then knowing that I wasn't. That it had nothing to do with politics or ideals. Of course, there were some with ideals. Not me. But I had conviction—you might even call it rare—the conviction to enlist at the Hotel Majestic on a stifling hot August day in 1944, when the war was already lost. Why I enlisted. I'm still not sure, but a reason was beside the point: It was a pure sacrifice, empty of reasons, a bigger, more grand self-erasure. On my way to enlist, I saw people shuttling into the Velo-drome. I won't deny that I saw them, being led inside. I was a helmeted dreamer who waited in a German uniform while Pétain dozed in his chambers. Pétain in his kepi with the scrambled eggs braid, who refused to see us, the few who were ready to keep going, the only people, correction, the only *person* with the conviction to fight to lose, to test nothing but extremes. They all caved and Pétain slept in his kepi with the scrambled eggs braid. I'm a man who had to go it alone, fight with conviction and for nothing, with men who didn't speak my language. The only one who didn't cave.

Fair enough, he thought. She's no more mysterious than I am to myself. And so here I am, in a burlesque club below the Tropic of Cancer, in this damp city where dreams are marbled with nothingness.

It was time for her show.

The blue lights flipped on. Smoky haze drifted above the tables.

"Introducing, from Paris, zazou dancer Rachel K!"